The White Raven, the Bear-King, and Other Grim Tales

by Manfred F. R. Kets de Vries

First published in 2016
By KDVI Press
Finsgate
5-7 Cranwood Street
London
United Kingdom
EC1V 9EE

www.kdvi.com

ISBN 978-0-9954948-1-7

A catalogue record for this book is available from the British Library.

A catalogue record for this book is available from the Library of Congress.

I wish to thank Philip Harris for the beauty of his drawings,
Sally Simmons for making the tales more "fairy-like,"
and Alicia Cheak for seeing the tales to the end.

Chapter 1

Introduction

We all know where we are with a fairy story. There is a cast of predictable characters (handsome prince, wicked stepmother, beautiful princess, the odd dragon, frog, or otherwise cursed beast, and so on). Our hero or heroine is submitted to terrible trials, cruelty and injustice but in the end the baddies get their comeuppance, good triumphs and everyone lives happily ever after.

Fairy tales provide a shortcut to a moral lesson, and reflections on human behavior. Their usefulness as a literary and psychological device has been recognized since the earliest times and has been perpetuated throughout our oral and written literary history, from Aesop's Fables in 600 BC, to the moral tales of La Fontaine in the 17th century and the Brothers Grimm in the 19th. These archetypical tales fulfill a basic therapeutic function-to reflect our deepest fears and desires and help us integrate them into a healthy personality.

Fairy tales explore the boundaries between reality and fantasy and between the animate and inanimate world. In fairy tales, the most amazing things happen: animals talk; people turn into animals; fairies are helpers; goblins create mischief; dragons and other monsters lie in wait for us; and there are miracles just around the corner. When we enter these "other worlds," there is the expectation that we will return to our own world with a new awareness, and with a new sense of energy, and hope.

The stimulus for this little book of fairy tales was an invitation to do a TED talk. The brevity of TED talks taught me something about the essence of storytelling. It also made me reflect on the stories I tell to my children and grandchildren. What messages did I want them to take away from my stories?

What are the values I want to convey? Nearly all fairy tales contain a specific, hidden message. Whatever the culture we live in, fairy tales teach us valuable life lessons. They put ordinary people in extraordinary situations. Their depictions of miraculous events, encounters, and experiences remain a valid part of the human experience. They are an invaluable part of our shared and personal history. With their symbolic language, the fairy tales that we first encounter in childhood retain their power over us, even as adults.

The TED talk motivated me to write five fairy tales to highlight some of the difficulties all of us face in our journey through life. What are some of the traps we should be aware of? How do we recognize the warning signs? The five tales in this book address a number of fundamental issues children (and adults) will encounter on their various life quests. We should know that only when we know what we want to do, and why we want to do it, would we be able to feel good about ourselves.

The first danger many of us are prone to is *lack of self-knowledge*. The question of knowing oneself has been with us since the dawn of time. This lack of self-knowledge may contribute to the second danger, that one of *hubris*. Some of us may become too arrogant and lose touch with reality and even self-destruct. The third danger concerns the *inability* of some of us *to get the best out of others*. Ineffective people fail to stretch others. They don't know how to make others better than they think that they can be. Linked to this human foible is a fourth one, pertaining to the *inability to work together*. To be effective we need to accept our personal limitations and surround ourselves with others who possess the strengths that we lack. This brings me to the fifth danger that culminates the other ones as it concerns humankind's ability to *create environments that are oppressive* for others.

The quests of the characters in these fairy tales in overcoming these human foibles should appeal to the hero or heroine in us all. I hope these stories will encourage us to embark on our own inner quest and make a difference in one way or another. Therefore, my intention has been that these tales should contain more than meets the eye, as well as entertain the reader.

In life, what really matters is that we have the chance to be what we are, and to become what we are capable of becoming. One of the greatest human fears is that at the end of our life we might discover that we have never really lived. We all have the urge to live fully, to do something significant, and to make a difference. Our biggest challenge is to work out how to do it. In writing this book of fairy tales I hope that it may provide the reader with a modicum of insight of how to make a difference- and in the process learn how to navigate five of the major challenges that they will encounter in life.

Chapter 2

The White Raven, or the King Who No Longer Knew Himself

Once upon a time there was a wise king, so beloved by his people, and so respected by all the neighboring kingdoms, that he was generally regarded as the greatest monarch alive. Under his rule, industry and fine arts flourished. The workers prospered and everyone was happy.

Now, it was well known that the king had a magic mirror that helped him rule so well. Every morning when he arose, the king would stand before the mirror. As he gazed at his reflection he could see his strengths and weaknesses; he could see his feet set firmly on the ground; he saw the problems he had to face and how to solve them; he saw the things that mattered and the things that were unimportant; he saw the decisions he had to take and how to take them. When he turned away from the mirror, the king felt confident that he would rule his kingdom justly, kindly and wisely.

But not everyone in the kingdom was happy. Deep in a cave in the darkest forest lived a wicked goblin that was eaten up with envy that the king was so adored by his subjects. As time went on, and the people grew happier, healthier and wealthier, the goblin's hatred grew wider and deeper.

One day, while the king was visiting his people in a distant part of the land, the wicked goblin crept into the palace, entered the king's bedroom, and put the magic mirror under a wicked spell. Laughing loudly, it said to itself, "Let's see how the king rules his kingdom, now!"

The next morning, the king awoke and went to the mirror as usual. But when he looked at the glass, something dreadful happened. He no longer recognized his reflection. Everything was distorted and confused. "Is this what I am really like?" the

king asked himself. "Is this my real self? Were all the other reflections false?" Day after day the mirror reflected someone who was a stranger to him. The king began to lose confidence in himself. He became very unhappy. He started to question the decisions he had made and changed his mind again and again, no longer sure that what he was doing was right. The king's confusion and doubt spread throughout the court. People began to wonder what had happened to their ruler. Now instead of being just, wise and benevolent he seemed weak, insecure and erratic. The discontent within the kingdom was music to the ears of the wicked goblin.

But after a while the king's subjects became used to their ruler's changed behavior. They said, "Things may not be as good as they were but they could be worse. Just look at the way other kingdoms are governed! Compared with them, we are not too badly off." This made the goblin very angry.

One day, when the king was in the throne room with his counselors, the goblin crept once more into the royal bedchamber, stole the magic mirror, and took it to the highest mountain in the land. At the summit, it held the mirror above its head, uttered a second spell, and threw it down the steepest cliff. When the mirror hit the ground it broke into millions of tiny pieces, which the wind picked up, blowing fragments of the cursed mirror into the eyes of every man, woman, and child in the kingdom.

From that moment on, all the king's subjects saw a distorted view of the world, as even the smallest splinters retained the power of the cursed mirror. With these chips of glass in their eyes, the king's people lost their sense of who they were. Like the king, they became strangers to themselves.

Faster than seemed possible, the kingdom that had been known for its wise, considerate, and just rule became a chaotic, unhappy place in which everyone had lost their grip on reality. The people no longer knew right from wrong. Where there had been harmony there was now discord, where happiness, sorrow. Gloating over the misery it had caused, the wicked goblin laughed and laughed until its belly shook.

Now a stranger to himself, the king's mood grew dark and somber and he withdrew more and more from his people. His despondency was contagious. Nobody laughed and people grew suspicious of their neighbors. They lost all sense of purpose and forgot how to do their work properly.

One night, the king had a terrifying dream. In his dream, he looked into the magic mirror and the sight of his own face filled him with dread. As he gazed in horror at his reflection, the mirror started to shake. It cracked into a million pieces that were carried by a strong wind into a dark cloud high up in the sky and from somewhere came the sound of malicious laughter. The king woke up, bathed in sweat, and summoned all his courtiers, crying, "Tell me the meaning of this terrible dream!" But none of his attendants could give him a satisfactory answer.

His courtiers' inability to help made the king even more despondent. With the horror of the dream still deeply etched in his mind, the king invited the wisest people in his kingdom to help him solve the riddle. But none of them could find the answer.

Finally, one of the courtiers told the king about a wise woman who lived in a land far, far away, and was known for her great knowledge. "Who knows?" the courtier said hesitantly. "She might be the one who could solve the riddle of your dream." When the king heard these words, he sent his most capable knight to fetch the wise woman, saying, "Ride day and night, and do whatever it takes, but bring this woman to my court without delay."

When the wise woman arrived at the court, the king recounted his dream. The woman listened carefully, then said, "Sire, the dream shows that someone has put a terrible curse on your kingdom."

The king asked the wise woman, "What can I do to make the kingdom well again?" "What can I do to recapture what we once had?" The woman replied, "The only way to break this spell is to find the potion of truth. But this will be a very difficult quest. It is only found in a far-off land. Anyone who tries to obtain it will be faced with grave dangers. Many have tried, but all have failed."

While the wise woman was speaking, the king's two sons were listening carefully. Now they stepped forward and said, "Please, father, give us your blessing to search for this rare potion. We will be honored to serve you and save the kingdom."

The king was very touched by their words but feared to lose his sons on such a dangerous expedition. But they continued to beg him to let them go. Finally, the king consented, and said, "Go, and my blessings upon the two of you. Because your quest is so important to everyone in our kingdom, the one who brings back this magic potion will be anointed as my successor."

Without delay, the two princes saddled their horses and galloped away. They journeyed night and day, crossing lakes, valleys, mountains, and other wild places in search of the magic potion.

The further the brothers went from the kingdom, the more clear-sighted they became, as the spell of the evil goblin began to lose its power. One day, completely exhausted from a long day's riding, they arrived at a crossing where two roads met. One road was wide, straight, and clear, while the other was narrow and overgrown. At the crossing was a sign that read:

Foolish traveler, beware!
Continue only if you dare.
Take the straight path: you might return.
The other's dangers you will learn.

The older prince said hastily, "I'll take the straight path," and before his brother could say a word, he galloped away. The younger prince realized that his brother had taken advantage of him, but he had no choice and took the narrow, overgrown path.

As night fell, the older prince arrived at a superb castle. He was very thankful to have reached such a place, as he was truly exhausted. As he dismounted, people who lit his way with torches greeted him warmly. They took his horse, and guided him through the entrance, which was richly decorated with precious stones and beautiful paintings. The prince was enchanted by such a reception after the hardships of his journey. "Finally," he thought, "I will be able to rest." But alas for the prince-what he did not know was that the beautiful castle was an illusion. In reality, he was in the wicked goblin's lair.

The prince entered a sumptuous hall, full of the sound of music and delicious smells. The tables were laden with so much food and wine that they were on the verge of collapsing. The prince fell on the food and drink hungrily. All around, beautiful women cast seductive glances at him and continued to fill his plate and glass.

The wicked goblin, disguised as a noble lord, welcomed him and gave him all the honors the prince could have wished for. Before long the prince had forgotten all about his quest for the magic potion. He felt very sleepy. "I never want to leave this wonderful place," he thought.

Meanwhile, the younger prince had taken the narrow, overgrown path and was on a very different journey. He traveled through snow-covered mountain passes, arid deserts, dangerous swamps, and treacherous rivers but, in spite of all the hardships, he pressed on. The promise he had made to his father weighed heavily on his mind. He was determined to complete the quest, whatever the cost.

Whenever the prince met people, he would ask them, "Tell me, please, where I can find the potion of truth." Every time, the answer was, "Far away, in a distant land, in a place where many dangers await you." But despite these discouraging replies, the prince did not give up.

One day, as the prince was riding through a deep, dark wood he heard a strange cry. After a long search, he came upon a beautiful white raven caught in a snare. To his great surprise, the bird spoke to him: "Please, my prince, set me free. An evil goblin has trapped me in this snare and if it finds me it will kill and eat me."

The prince, who was very kind at heart, freed the bird. The white raven spread its wings and prepared to fly but as it did so said, "Dear prince, I am forever in your debt. You have saved my life. Is there anything that I can do for you? Let me know your heart's desire." The prince said, "Please help me to find the potion of truth. I have looked for it far and wide, but it is nowhere to be found."

The raven replied, "Dear prince, I will help you but you must listen very carefully. Not far from here, in the deepest part of this dark, dangerous wood, you will find a castle. You should enter this castle but beware. The castle is just an illusion. In truth, it's the lair of a wicked goblin. This goblin has caused me great suffering and is also responsible for the misery that has visited your father's kingdom. Therefore, be cautious. Do not eat or drink anything you are offered or you will fall into a deep sleep and be unable to complete your quest. So just feign that you are doing so. When everyone is asleep tonight, I will come and find you. I will lead you to a magic sword which is the only weapon that can kill the goblin. You must cut off its head, and then you will find the potion of truth among its treasure in the cave."

When the prince arrived at the castle, it was just as the white raven had told him. Delicious food and wine were put before him, but the prince only pretended to eat and drink. The same beautiful women smiled at him and the prince just smiled back. After a while, the prince laid down and pretended to be fast asleep.

When the castle was completely silent the prince heard the sound of wings and the white raven appeared. As it had promised, the bird guided him to the magic sword, which the prince fastened to his belt. Then he followed the raven into the depths of the cave, from which strange sounds were coming. It was the evil goblin, fast asleep and snoring loudly. With one great thrust

of the sword the prince cut off its ugly head. The raven then flew to a shelf in the farthest corner, where the prince found the phial containing the potion of truth. As he put it safely in his pack, he heard desperate cries and loud banging even deeper in the cave. There he found his unfortunate brother, imprisoned in a dungeon. Another great thrust of the magic sword sliced through the heavy lock and the brothers fell into one another's arms.

Saying farewell to the white raven, the two princes set off on the long journey home. But as they traveled, the older prince grew more and more quiet and withdrawn. He was deeply ashamed that he had fallen for the evil goblin's tricks and failed in the quest to find the potion of truth. Now, he remembered what their father had said as he gave them his blessing: his younger brother would inherit the kingdom.

His heart was torn with envy. As they got nearer to the kingdom, the older prince determined to kill his brother and steal the potion. He would tell his father that his brother had died bravely but that he was the one who had successfully completed the quest. He would be named the future king. As they drew close to home, the older prince looked for an opportunity to murder his brother and take the magic phial.

One day, as they rested near a well, the older prince saw that his chance had come. He told his brother that he could hear a raven calling from deep in the well. His brother said he could hear nothing. "Come closer to the well," said the older prince. The younger prince approached but could still hear nothing. "I fear it is our friend the white raven," said the older prince. At this, the younger prince ran to the well and leaned over to try to see the bird. As he did so, his brother pushed him as hard as he could and the poor prince tumbled in. Without looking back, the older prince took the potion from his brother's pack, jumped on his horse, and rode towards the kingdom.

When he reached the castle, the first thing his father asked was, "Where is your brother? Why isn't he here? What happened to him?"

"Alas, father," said the prince, "we came to a crossing and my brother took the way of no return. After we parted, I saw him no more. But despite the many hardships that lay before me, I succeeded in obtaining the potion of truth."

On hearing this news, the king cried with joy that the spell that hung over the kingdom could now be broken. But he also shed many tears over the loss of his younger son, and cherished the secret hope that he might still be alive.

And indeed he was. The well into which he had been pushed was dry, and filled with soft leaves that broke his fall. For many hours the younger prince called for help, hoping that a passing traveler might hear him. After some time, a traveler did stop by, hoping to water his horse. When he heard the desperate cries coming from deep in the well, he lowered a rope, and helped the prince out. Thanking his rescuer from the bottom of his heart, the younger prince went on his way to the kingdom.

When he arrived at his father's castle, there was great joy throughout the land. But the king turned red with anger when the prince told his father how his older brother had robbed him of the potion and tried to kill him. "How could he do such a vile thing to his brother?" cried the king. "He will die for this."

But the young prince pleaded with his father to spare his brother's life and eventually softened the old man's heart.

Instead, the older prince was banished from the kingdom. Where he went, nobody knew-and nobody ever cared.

The king told the prince what the wise woman had decreed should be done with the potion of truth. "Climb to the top of the mountain behind the castle. When you reach the summit, open the phial and cast the potion of truth into the wind. It will be blown throughout the kingdom and the spell of the wicked goblin will be broken."

To his great surprise, when the prince reached the summit of the mountain, he saw the white raven soaring high above him. As the prince opened the phial, the bird swooped down from the sky, snatched it from the prince's hand, and rose high on the wind, scattering the precious potion as it flew. Then the bird dropped to earth at the feet of the prince and before his eyes transformed into a beautiful princess-the loveliest woman the prince had ever seen.

As the drops of potion were spread through the sky, it was as if a dark cloud had lifted from the land. All over the kingdom people suddenly felt transformed. They were no longer strangers to themselves. And the king realized that he no longer needed the magic mirror to know how to rule wisely and well.

Princess White Raven told the prince that when the potion of truth had lifted the curse that was on the kingdom, it had also broken the spell that the wicked goblin had put on her and enabled her to return to her true form. The prince, having proven himself to the White Raven by lifting the curse, had won her heart. In due course, they were married, eventually ruling the kingdom with clear-sightedness and compassion.

Chapter 3

The Bear-King

Once upon a time, in the middle of a deep, dark forest in a land far, far away stood the palace of a king who ruled over an immense empire. But although his kingdom was rich and powerful, all was not well. The people were not happy and laughter was never heard in the land.

The king was a cold, proud man. Although he had conquered all the neighboring countries, he was still dissatisfied. Instead of being kind, fair and wise, he was cruel, arrogant and arbitrary. Nobody lived up to his unrealistic expectations. However hard people worked and tried to please him, they were met with sarcasm and ridicule. If they made even the slightest mistake, the king's rage was devastating. He never forgave or forgot an error or a negative comment. Once, when one of his oldest and most loyal advisors warned him that the people were unhappy and suffering hardships, the king erupted in uncontrollable rage. "Get out of my sight!" he commanded. "If you enter my court again I will have your head!" As the old man left, the king turned to his attendants and said, "Follow him and see that he leaves with nothing but the clothes on his back. Seize his gold and his lands and burn down his house. He will learn what it means to criticize the king."

After this, nobody dared bring the king any bad news. They made sure he only heard the things he wanted to hear. No matter what disasters befell parts of his empire, every day they would report, "All is well, everywhere." Terrified of provoking the king's anger and malice, they flattered and complimented him from dawn to dusk.

But of course, affairs in the kingdom were far from well. While the king's self-importance increased daily, his tyrannical rule was taking its toll. The harvests failed, trade declined, and his people grew poor and hungry. But the king's counselors did not dare tell him the truth about his errors of judgment and the mistakes he made. Soon, the prosperous and powerful kingdom was full of misery and discontent but the king, surrounded by flatterers in his sumptuous palace, saw none of it.

Many of the king's subjects decided to leave the country to find a better life elsewhere. Fishermen, farmers, masons, teachers, judges, and courtiers-everyone with a skill and a mind of their own settled in neighboring kingdoms that were ruled wisely and well. Those who were too fearful to leave and had to remain did so with a heavy heart.

When the king began to ask where his people had gone, his courtiers panicked. How could they tell him that the best and brightest in the land were leaving because of his cruelty and neglect? Instead, they told him, "Sire, they have left the kingdom because they realized that they were not good enough to stay." And the king would reply, "Good riddance."

Eventually, as the power of the empire began to fall away, people in the conquered territories seized the chance to rebel. Worse, many of the generals and politicians who had fled the kingdom now helped lead the rebel lands. The king's rage when he saw this pushed him to extreme vindictiveness. He condemned his disloyal generals to death and his subjects grew even more afraid of him.

The king's courtiers now found that flattery and compliments were no longer enough to satisfy their ruler and began to despair. Then one of his attendants said, "Perhaps the king is lonely. Perhaps he needs a wife. A wife might help him to be more compassionate and merciful. If we hold a ball and invite the most beautiful women in the land, perhaps he will find a wife among them."

The courtiers were clever, and told the king that they wanted to organize a ball to celebrate his rule. The ball would show what a magnificent king he really was and make the rulers of the rebel kingdoms jealous. Pleased with this idea, the king gave them his blessing.

Despite the misery of their daily life, news of the ball lifted the spirits of many throughout the kingdom. Such celebrations had been few and far between. Everyone who counted for anything in the kingdom was sent an invitation, as were the nobility in the surrounding countries. The courtiers made sure that there would be hundreds of princesses, duchesses, marquises, viscountesses, baronesses, and noble ladies in attendance. Surely the king would fall for one of them? Surely there would be a woman among so many who could soften the king's heart?

The day of the ball came and everything was grand, luxurious, and resplendent. But the king's reaction was far from what his courtiers had hoped. None of the women he met was good enough for him; none of them was perfect; they all had at least one major fault. "She's ugly, she's fat, she's too thin, she's too tall, she's too short, her nose is crooked, her teeth stick out, she's too old, she's even older, she's wearing a wig, her feet are enormous. I deserve better than this."

One young woman in particular captivated everyone at the ball with her beauty and modesty. But the king seemed oblivious to her charms, even though it was clear to all the

others that the young woman had very tender feelings for the king. When the courtiers introduced her, she shyly presented him with a gift-a cloak in a hundred different colors that she had woven herself. But the king merely said, "What use is this rag to me?" and rising to his feet, he tossed the beautiful cloak to one side and strode out of the room, out of the palace and into the woods beyond.

In the cool of the forest that surrounded the palace, the king's rage began to subside. After wandering for some time he arrived at a deep, clear pool, fed by a spring and sparkling in the moonlight. Without a second's thought, the king threw off his clothes and slipped into the cooling water. But when he clambered out, quite refreshed, he found to his great irritation that his royal garments had disappeared. Furious, the king wondered who would dare steal his clothes. Who could have been so impertinent? He would have his head for it! But meanwhile, what could he do? How could he return to the palace without any clothes?

While he was trying to work out what to do next, the king heard a rustle in the undergrowth and then ominous growling. There, making its way around the pool towards him was an enormous bear. The old animal was filthy, ragged and starving and had clearly decided that the king would be its next meal. The king had no weapon to defend himself and was filled with fear. He was going to die and be eaten by this repulsive animal. Would that really be his end? Here, where nobody would find him, rather than as he had always imagined, in his stately palace, surrounded by his devoted followers and grieved by an entire empire? The idea was intolerable.

Just when all hope seemed to be lost, suddenly, out of nowhere, a stranger appeared. The king cried out to him, pleading, "Help me, please, save me!" The stranger called back, "I will help you, great king, but only if you grant me a wish." "Whatever you like!" screamed the king, who could feel the bear's hot breath on his face.

Immediately he spoke, the stranger jumped before the bear, and with one sweep of his sword killed the beast. Then, ripping off the bear's mangy coat, he said to the king, "Great king, to cover your bare skin, I will give you another. This bearskin will be all your covering, your coat and blanket as well. My wish, having saved your life, is that you wear this bearskin from this day forth. Wherever you go, this new coat will go with you." And as he spoke, he threw the bearskin over the king's head and it stuck like glue to the king's body.

The king gave a great cry and tried to struggle out from under the dirty, smelly pelt. "Give me back my robes!" he demanded. But the stranger said, "Do not exhaust yourself. You will wear this coat until you learn what it truly means to be a king and how to rule so that your people are happy and prosperous." As the king stood and cursed him the stranger disappeared before his eyes.

Despite the stranger's words, the king continued to try to tear off the bearskin but it was hopeless. The skin fitted him as if it was his own. He ran towards the pool, thinking he might wash it off, but stopped when he saw his reflection in the water. Dark, dirty hair covered his face, his teeth were yellow and menacing, his eyes were small, black and mean looking and his fingers ended in claws.

Nevertheless, the Bear-King decided to return to the palace. He was sure that, when he addressed his guards, they would recognize his voice and let him in. Then he would assemble his greatest counselors to find a way to lift the stranger's curse.

But when the guards saw the strange creature approaching the palace gate, they threw sticks and stones at it to drive it away. When the Bear-King called out to them, saying "I am your king, let me into my palace," they fell about laughing, a sound that had not been heard in the kingdom for many years. "Why, your majesty," they mocked, "how delightful you look and how sweet you smell! This is certainly the way to find a wife! Now get along, you monster, and if you return we will kill you."

The Bear-King was outraged. How dare they laugh at him! How dare they make fun of him! How dare they say he was ugly and smelled!

Chased away by his guards, the king had no choice but to roam the land. But everywhere he went, the sight of him terrified the people he encountered. Just a short time before he had been the most feared and powerful person in the kingdom; now he was a monster, turned away from people's homes, threatened and abused. As he wandered from place to place, the Bear-King began to realize how much misery he had caused his people. Everywhere he went, he saw how little food and money they had and how suspicious they were of each other. And nobody had a good word for the king. In fact they blamed his arrogance and self-regard for all their troubles. "One monster in the kingdom is enough," they said, as they beat the Bear-King away from their villages.

"How selfish I have been!" thought the Bear-King now. "I believed everyone loved me but they fear and despise me. There is no kindness and pity in my kingdom because I drove it out with my own cruelty. I ruled my people when I should have served them. I do not deserve any better than this." So it was that the king's old arrogance began to melt away and he grew humble, gentle and kind. "When I looked like a king, I was a monster inside," sighed the Bear-King. "Now I have become a monster but know what a king should be. How strange life is, when a curse becomes a blessing."

As time went on, the Bear-King grew used to his life as an outcast. He took work where he found it-often nasty, dirty work that no one else would do-and slept and sheltered where he could. Although his monstrous appearance did not change and some people still ran away from him in fear, others realized that he was no danger to them and he met many acts of kindness. When people were cruel and mocked him, he was reminded of his old ways and vowed never to be that king again. When people pitied him and gave him food and shelter, he vowed to be like them if he was ever free from the curse and king again. When he had food and money to spare, he gave it to those who were worse off than himself and with each gift made a wish that his good actions might help lift the curse. He was no longer bitter about his strange fate. Instead he made the best of what he had and what he could do and was glad to feel strong and able to work hard to help other people.

One night, after he had been wandering for a very long time, the Bear-King took shelter in a cave. He was very hungry as he had nothing to eat for several days apart from roots and berries he gathered in the forest. In the cave he found a massive wooden chest, carved with an intricate design and thick with dust. When the Bear-King lifted the lid, abundant gold and precious stones tumbled out. The Bear-King marveled at his good fortune. "I will return to the inn I passed on my way here," he told himself, "and buy myself a good dinner and a warm bed for the night."

But, as had happened so many times before, when the Bear-King knocked at the door of the inn, the innkeeper refused to let him in, as his appearance would frighten the other guests. However, when the Bear-King showed her some of his gold, the innkeeper's attitude changed. "You can sleep in the stable and I hope you won't frighten the horses," she said. But she made the Bear-King promise not to let himself be seen by the other guests. "You may as well clean the stable, too," she added. "It's filthy and I can't get anyone to do the job." The Bear-King readily agreed to this, as he was used to doing the kind of work that nobody wanted.

By the time the innkeeper brought him his food, the Bear-King had cleared, swept, scrubbed and polished the stable and strewn fresh, sweet straw to sleep on. But as he lay down to rest, he heard soft weeping outside the stable door. Quietly, he rose and saw an old man who was sobbing bitterly. Catching sight of the Bear-King, the old man gave a cry of fright and tried to run away. But the Bear-King spoke kindly to him and invited the old man into the warm, clean stable to rest and tell him the cause of all his sorrow.

The old man told the Bear-King that he was a nobleman who had fallen out of favor with the king. He had tried to warn the king that things were not going well in the kingdom-that people were poor and unhappy and planning to leave. But the king had not appreciated his honesty. He had thrown the old man out of the palace, confiscated all his belongings and burned down his house. Now the old man was reduced to begging for food and drink. "I am old and tired," sobbed the old man, "and cannot go on much longer. Then what will become of my three poor daughters? They will starve."

The Bear-King was full of sorrow when he realized that he had been the cause of all the old man's misery. "If this is your only problem, I can help you," he said. "I have money enough." And he put a bag of gold into the poor man's hand.

The old man was beside himself with happiness and gratitude and demanded that the Bear-King tell him what he could do for him in return. The Bear-King sighed. "I am very lonely," he said, "but look at me-who will want to give me their company?"

"I shall!" said the old man straight away. "You shall come and stay with me and my daughters. It is little more than a hovel but we will make room for you. You will no longer be lonely. At my home, you shall find the companionship that you seek."

The Bear-King was overjoyed at the old man's words. Might he have a chance of ending his solitude and finding acceptance amongst others? He accepted the old man's offer and followed him to his lodging.

When the two arrived, the old man thought it wise to ask the Bear-King to wait outside while he told his daughters what he had promised. While the old man was explaining what had happened, the oldest girl looked through the window and saw

the Bear-King. Screaming, she ran out and hid in the garden. The second daughter then looked through the window and said, "How can you suggest this monster live with us, father? He is far too ugly to have around every day." With that, she slipped away and hid in the cellar.

However, his youngest daughter said, "Father, from all you have told us, this creature must have a very good heart. A good heart counts for more than good looks. I will be very happy to invite him into our home." With this she opened the door and asked the Bear-King to come inside.

When the Bear-King saw the young woman, he recognized her straight away. She was the girl who had offered him the beautiful cloak at the ball. He remembered that he had thrown it away and not even thanked her. Now he saw that she was beautiful as well as kind. How could he not have noticed this when he first met her? He considered how ugly, vile and dirty he now appeared. "Why doesn't she run away like the others?" he asked himself. "Why is she willing to let me in?" When the young woman approached him, smiling, and offered him a glass of wine, he could not help asking, "How can you bear to look at a monster like me?" The young woman replied, "You are not a monster. I see someone who is kind, generous, and sensitive to the suffering of others. I see someone with a noble heart."

The Bear-King was deeply touched by her words. This lovely young woman saw past his ugly face and hideous, hairy body to the true, good heart within. It was then that he fell in love with her. But how could he ask this sweet girl to marry him while the stranger's curse lay upon him? Sighing, he told her: "I wish to remain with you and your father but I cannot. I have to leave you now, but take this ring and keep it as a reminder of me. I have another just like it and I will look at it and shine it every day and remember you. When I am ready, I will return and we will be reunited." Then the Bear-King slipped the ring on her finger and went on his way.

The youngest daughter was very unhappy to see the Bear-King leave and her eyes filled with tears. Her sisters did nothing to comfort her. Indeed, they mocked and teased her. "How can you have affection for such a monster? Nobody will believe that you love him. Everyone will laugh at you." But the youngest daughter did her best to ignore her unkind sisters and when she looked at the Bear-King's ring and shone the beautiful jewel that was set in it, she whispered a wish to herself, "Keep him safe until he returns to me."

By now, a year had passed since the stranger had saved the king's life in the forest and transformed him with the curse that had strangely proved to be a blessing. The Bear-King decided to return to the sparkling pool where his transformation had taken place. Perhaps the stranger knew about his hard work and acts of charity and his fervent wishes for the spell to be broken. When the Bear-King arrived at the pool, he called out to the stranger, "Are you there? Here am I once more and greatly changed." There was a rush of wind and the stranger stood before him. "You look much the same to me," he said. "How is it that you are changed?" The Bear-King replied, "I have wandered through this kingdom and learned about pride and cruelty, poverty and hardship. I have learned about kindness and pity, charity and humility. Thanks to you, I have learned that a curse can prove to be a blessing and that a humble heart is worth more than a king's crown." As the Bear-King said these words, the spell was broken, the dirty bearskin fell from his body, and his royal robes reappeared by the side of the pool.

The king turned to thank the stranger once more but he had disappeared. Putting on his splendid clothes, the king set out for the palace. When he arrived at the gates, the same sentries were there who had thrown sticks and stones at him and driven him away. Seeing the king approach, they threw the gates open wide and cried, "Your majesty! You are safe! Did you not see the hideous beast that was just here? He claimed to be king and tried to enter the palace. We were afraid he had done you harm!" And so the king learned that the stranger's spell had made it seem that he had never been away.

The ball had finished, the noble guests had left and the palace was quiet. As the king made his way to his chamber, he noticed how people shrank from him and turned their heads away in fear, just as people had turned in terror from the Bear-King. His heart was heavy with remorse and shame; now he looked like a king but people only saw a monster. "I will make amends," he swore to himself. "I will show my people that I am properly humbled. I will show them that I have learned to love them and despise my former self."

The next day, the king took to his throne and called his four most loyal counselors to him. To each he gave a purse full of gold and told them, "Take this gold and go out into the kingdom, to the north, south, east, and west. Help the farmers to till the land and sow their crops. Help the masons to repair the bridges and the people's cottages. See that the drudges who clear, sweep, scrub, and polish have food and clothing and somewhere to sleep. Whenever you see a man or woman giving alms to a beggar, give that person five times what they gave and tell them they have the blessing of their king. And if you come upon a poor creature who looks neither man nor beast and nothing so much as a monster, give it food and shelter because you will find it has a good heart."

The people were full of wonder. How their king had changed! Now he no longer scowled, raged or threatened. Now he smiled and asked his courtiers for advice and listened to what they said. Now he greeted his subjects when he passed them in the palace or rode through the streets. He stopped to admire and praise their work, their homes, their vegetable gardens, and their orchards. "Why, we thought he was a proud and heartless monster," the people said to each other. "But he has shown us that he has a warm and caring heart."

One day, seeing that matters of state were now in order, the king called for the royal carriage with its eight white horses to be brought to him and told his coachmen to drive to the old man's cottage. The old man began to tremble with fear when he saw his oppressor's carriage at his door and with great trepidation invited the king to enter. Imagine his bewilderment when the king greeted him gently, asked after his health and for his permission to sit down, and praised the neatness and comfort of his home. The old man could barely stammer his gratitude for the king's changed nature, then asked what he could do for the king. To his amazement, the king asked to meet his three daughters. "I know that they are very beautiful," he said, "and I would like to ask one of your daughters to be my queen." The old man went swiftly to fetch them.

When the two oldest daughters heard who their visitor was and why he had come they pulled on their finest dresses and rushed to greet him. They elbowed and pinched and stamped on each others' feet in an effort to be the first to offer the king wine and delicious things to eat. The king thanked them politely but barely noticed their smiles and simpering and attempts to flatter. He was looking for the youngest daughter but she remained in the kitchen, in her shabbiest dress, longing for the Bear-King.

Finally, the king grew impatient and said, "Old man, where is your youngest daughter?" "Oh, sire," said the oldest sister, "you have no need to meet her. She does nothing but toil and mope and weep by the kitchen fire." "Worse," said the second sister, "she toils and mopes and weeps for a hideous monster that she loves." But the king would not be refused and commanded the old man to fetch his youngest daughter and bring her to him.

When she entered the room and saw the king, the youngest daughter curtsied deeply, not daring to look at him. She trembled because of her old dress and the smuts on her face then trembled even more as the king reached out and took one of her careworn hands. Into her palm he dropped a golden ring, burnished bright with a sparkling jewel. It was the exact same ring that she wore on her finger and that the Bear-King had given her before he left! How had it come into the possession of the king? Torn between hope and fear, she gazed into the king's face.

"Yes," said the king, "I am the wretched monster that you invited in. A curse was put upon me because of my arrogance and cruelty and I roamed my kingdom as an outcast for a long while. But my curse became a blessing because I learned the value of humility, modesty and a good heart. And when I had learned that lesson, I regained my human form and became a king once more."

With this, the king took the youngest daughter in his arms. When her sisters realized that the king they had just been flattering was the beast-like monster they had ridiculed, they ran out of the house in shame.

Who can doubt what happened next? The king married his queen; happiness, prosperity and laughter spread throughout the land; and the people, like the king and queen, lived happily ever after.

Chapter 4

The Mysterious Crone

Once upon a time, there was a woman who had two daughters. One daughter was very beautiful and industrious but the other was ugly and lazy. Yet of the two, the woman loved the ugly, lazy girl best, because she was her own daughter. The ugly, lazy daughter was treated like a princess but the stepdaughter was made to work like a servant in the house. No household task, big or small, that the stepdaughter completed was ever good enough. Her stepmother scolded and criticized. "Don't do it like that!" she would say. "Do it again, and this time do it properly!" Yet she never explained what the girl had done wrong or how she could do it better.

Life was very hard for the stepdaughter. She never had enough to eat and she had so many chores to do that she barely had time to sleep. While her sister was given the most delicious things on the table, the stepdaughter had to make do with leftovers. She had only rags to wear, while her sister wore the finest clothes made from the best fabrics that could be found. When her sister sat and showed off her finery in the parlor, the stepdaughter was banished to the kitchen. Her stepmother would say, "Who wants that bundle of rags in the parlor? Let her stay in the kitchen and do an honest day's work, dirty, lazy child."

The poor stepdaughter had to rise while it was still dark to carry the water from the well, collect firewood, light the stove, begin the cooking and do the washing. It was dark again before all her work was done. If that were not enough work, her stepmother and stepsister would torment her all day, finding fault, inventing extra tasks and chivvying her to do everything faster. At night, she had no bed, but had to lie down by the fire

among the ashes. Although her stepmother never thanked or praised her, the poor girl did everything as best she could.

One day, when the fall had come, and there had been lots of rain, the woman told her stepdaughter to go out into the forest and collect wild mushrooms. She gave her precise instructions about which direction to take and threatened her with all kinds of punishment if she went the wrong way and failed to bring any mushrooms back with her. But in fact the stepmother had planned for her stepdaughter to get lost deep in the forest where there were wild animals that would tear her to pieces. "And not before time," the wicked woman said to herself. "It will be one less mouth to feed."

Following her stepmother's directions closely, the girl stepped into the forest, looking everywhere for the precious mushrooms. But she could not see a single one and all the time the way was taking her deeper and deeper into the gloomy depths of the forest. The withered leaves crackled under her feet and the bare branches wound so thickly together that no sun penetrated to the forest floor. Soon, the girl realized that she was lost. It grew darker and darker, the wind rose with a sound like the howling of wolves, and a heavy rain began to fall, wetting her to the bone. But still the poor girl went on, saying to herself, "I must find the wild mushrooms for Stepmother."

Eventually, she could walk no further and sank down on a log to rest. "What am I to do?" she wept. "How will I find my way home? And how can I return to Stepmother without any mushrooms? She will be so angry and cruel to me." As she wept, she caught sight of a little red snake that was struggling to free itself from a stone that had fallen on its tail. "Poor little snake, let me help you," the girl said. Quickly, she lifted the stone, and the snake slithered happily away.

Summoning all that remained of her strength, the girl set off again, still looking on all sides for the wild mushrooms. Suddenly, she heard a rustling sound in the leaves that were strewn around her. There was a small red turtle, lying on its back and struggling futilely to roll onto its legs. "Poor little turtle, let me help you," she said, and gave the turtle a firm push. Righted, the turtle waggled away merrily.

On she walked until, further ahead, the girl heard a bird singing so beautifully that her spirits were instantly lifted. Following the sound, she arrived at a clearing in the forest where a beautiful red bird was sitting on the branch of a tree, singing with all its heart. In her entire life, the girl had never heard such a beautiful sound. As she listened, the bird spread its wings and glided away. As if under a spell, the girl followed the bird even deeper into the forest. Just as she thought she could go no further, she saw lights glimmering in the darkness and to her great surprise, between the massive trunks of two trees she saw an entrance, lit by flaming torches, with a gate standing open. On it sat the beautiful red bird.

"Did you bring me here, Bird?" asked the girl. The bird merely cocked its head at her. I'm so tired, thought the girl. Perhaps here I will find somewhere to rest for a while. "Shall I go in, Bird?" she asked again but again the bird just fixed her with a shining eye. "Well, I shall," said the girl stoutly. "I can always turn back if anything goes wrong." She passed through the gate and found herself in the large, beautifully decorated hall of a little castle.

As she stood wondering where exactly she was and what to do next, she heard the sound of footsteps coming in her direction. Out of the shadows appeared an old, old woman with very thin legs, a big nose and sharp, metal teeth. The girl was terrified and turned to run away, but the crone called after her, "What are you afraid of, dear child? Stay with me. You must be hungry and tired. I will give you good food to eat and work to do. If you work well for me, I will see that you are not unhappy." The crone spoke so kindly, despite looking so frightening, that the girl thanked her and agreed to enter into her service.

The crone led the girl to a table spread with good things and told her to eat and drink to her heart's content. Then she said, "I have a large herd of cows and a very large barn to keep them safe from wolves and bears. But I no longer have the strength to bring the cows in for milking. Could you do this for me?"

Without any hesitation, the girl took a long stick and a milking stool, and went out to the meadow to fetch the cows in. And in no time, the barn was full of mooing cows and the sweet smell of fresh milk. The crone was overjoyed, and praised the girl for working so well.

When the milking was finished, the crone said, "I have promised the troll that lives in the middle of this forest some yarn to make blankets for the winter. Would you help me spin my yarn?" The girl was eager to show the kind old woman what she could do and in no time several large skeins of yarn lay at the crone's feet. Again, the crone was delighted and praised the girl for her work.

Then the crone said, "I have invited all the trolls in the forest for tea and promised them jam tarts but I have no dough.

Can you help me?" And in no time, the girl had rolled up her sleeves, measured, mixed, leveled, cut, and baked the dough and the kitchen was filled with the smell of warm jam tarts. Again, the crone marveled and praised her for her work.

From this time on, the girl took care to do everything that the crone asked, as the old woman treated her so kindly and looked after her so well. The crone never spoke angrily, even when she made a mistake, but showed her how things should be done. If things didn't work out as expected, she would explain how the girl could have done them differently. And every day, the crone gave the girl the most delicious things to eat and drink. Soon the girl began to notice ways in which she could make the crone's castle even more comfortable. Without being asked, she beat and washed the carpets, sewed new curtains to keep the winter winds out, picked and preserved the late fruit from the orchard, fattened the geese ready for feast days, and prepared the vegetable plot for planting in the spring. And whenever the crone saw the girl going about these self-appointed tasks, she would thank, praise and encourage her. And every time the crone praised and thanked her, the young woman resolved to do the best she could for her.

The young woman was very happy in the little castle in the forest and stayed with the crone for a long time. But after a while she began to be troubled. She had not picked the wild mushrooms her stepmother had asked for. Her stepmother and stepsister must think that she was lost or worse, torn to pieces by bears or wolves. They would be angry and worried. Even though the girl was a thousand times happier with the crone than with her stepmother and stepsister, she felt that she had to return home.

When she said this to the crone, the old woman didn't seem surprised and replied, "I am very grateful for the way you have served me all this time, so well and so faithfully. You always give your best and everything you have done for me has made me very happy. And you have a heart of gold. Do you remember that on your way here you helped a snake and a turtle that were in trouble, even though you were in great trouble yourself? I know about these things-the red bird sang them to me.

"To reward you for all the good things you have done for me and others, I will give you this magic cloak and this magic bow. Every time you put your hand in a pocket of the cloak you will find what you deserve. Every time you aim this bow, its arrows will find their mark."

Then the crone took the girl by the hand to the castle entrance between the two tree trunks. The gate closed behind her and the girl immediately found herself back on the edge of the wood by her stepmother's house.

The girl put her left hand in the pocket of the cloak and pulled out a handful of fresh wild mushrooms. But when she put her right hand in the other pocket, she pulled it out full of gold. The same thing happened again and again. The girl realized that the crone had helped her to riches and freedom from the tyranny of her wicked stepmother. Stepping into the kitchen where she had spent so many miserable days and nights, she laid the mushrooms on the table and slipped away again without being seen.

The girl used her new fortune wisely. She helped so many people with her magical wealth that she became known far and wide. Even the king came to hear of her kindness, industry, and generosity and so, of course, did her stepmother and stepsister.

"There she is, helping all and sundry, and what has she done for us?" snapped the stepmother. "After everything I gave her-food for her greedy stomach and a roof over her ungrateful head. All she left us was a pile of mushrooms. I will bring her here and make her tell us all."

The stepmother was clever and sent the girl an affectionate message and gave her a warm welcome when she arrived. But after talking for a while, she could not help bursting out, "How is it possible that you are so rich? Tell me at once!"

When the stepmother heard the story of how the girl had found the castle in the forest and worked for the crone and been given the magic cloak and bow, she thought to herself, "Why shouldn't my real daughter have the same? Why shouldn't she go to live with the crone and become rich? Why should my stepdaughter have all this gold? It's not fair!"

The stepmother ordered her daughter to go into the forest and find the crone. "You needn't stay long," she said. "Just do what you're told for a while, then tell her you're sick for home and want to leave. She will give you the magic cloak and bow and then we will be as rich as your foolish sister." But her daughter was not easy to persuade. "I don't want to go and work for that witch and ruin my nice clothes milking cows and spinning thread and making tarts for horrid trolls," she said. But her mother nagged and bullied, and finally got her way.

With great reluctance, the lazy daughter entered the forest, grumbling all the while. Soon she came upon a little red snake that was caught beneath a rock. "Ugh!" exclaimed the stepsister. "How I hate snakes! I hope it hurries up and dies!" And she walked on, leaving the snake writhing in misery. Later she spied a little red turtle that lay helplessly on its back. The lazy daughter laughed as the poor creature waved its legs and rolled from side to side. "Good luck, you silly animal!" she called as she went on her way. But when she heard the red bird singing, she remembered to do as her sister had done and followed it to the magic gate that led to the little castle.

Unlike her sister, the lazy daughter knew what to expect when the hideous crone appeared, and showed no sign of fear at the sight of her. She accepted the crone's offer of a place in her household and, like her sister, was given the task of bringing the cows in from the field and milking them. At first, she made an effort to exert herself, thinking about all the gold she would get in return, but she quickly gave up and the barn was full of the bellows of unhappy cows, desperate to be milked. "Dear madam," she said to the crone, "You must see that this is no job for me, with my leather slippers and silk gown. Perhaps you have another task that will suit me better?"

But when the crone asked the lazy daughter to help to spin the yarn for the goblin's blankets, she made a half-hearted attempt to turn the spindle and quickly gave up. "Alas, this is no job for me," she told the crone. "The yarn burns my fingers and my arms ache so much. Is there no other task I can do?"

So the crone took the lazy daughter to the kitchen and explained that dough was needed for the trolls' jam tarts. "My dear madam!" laughed the girl. "Eating pastry is one thing but making it? I'm afraid this is no job for me." The same thing happened with all the other tasks that the crone gave the lazy daughter to do and in the end the crone tired of the lazy daughter long before the girl herself was ready to ask to leave.

When the crone agreed that the lazy daughter could go back to her old world, the girl was delighted, and thought to herself, "Soon I will have the magic cloak and pockets full of gold."

The crone led the lazy daughter to the hidden gateway and, as the girl expected, handed her a cloak and bow, saying, "This is in return for your services. Both will give you what you deserve." The girl stepped through the gate and was overjoyed to find herself at home again. Eagerly, she thrust her hands into the pockets of the cloak, but when she pulled out her left hand it was full of dust and when she pulled out her right hand it was full of sand. The same thing happened again and again but still there was no gold. The lazy daughter shrieked with rage and bitterness.

Now, while the lazy daughter had been away with the crone a dragon had entered the kingdom and begun to roam the countryside, devouring the people's sheep and cattle and carrying children away in its claws to be eaten in its lair.

The people implored the king to help them but none of his counselors could tell him what needed to be done. Although many of his brave knights had tried to slay the dragon, they too had been carried away and eaten. The king sent his messengers out through the land to proclaim that the person who succeeded in killing the dragon would have anything in the kingdom that he or she wanted.

The stepmother had been furious that the magic cloak given to her favorite daughter had not made them rich, but now she saw another opportunity to obtain fame and riches-the lazy daughter still had the magic bow. Handing the girl a quiver of arrows, she pushed her out into the fields to await the dragon's next raid, saying, "I know this sort of magic—it works every time. Just loose the arrows and kill the dragon and the king will make us the richest people in the land."

Sure enough, the dragon swept down from its lair, hoping to grab its next meal. The lazy daughter took an arrow from the quiver, drew her bow, and aimed straight at the dragon. But to her dismay, instead of hitting the dragon, the arrow made a complete circle and landed with a thud in the turf at her feet! Again and again the desperate girl took an arrow, drew her bow and aimed but each time the arrow flew straight back to where she stood. The dragon, angered that someone was trying to harm it, flew down, grabbed the lazy daughter in its claws, and took her to its lair, ready for its next meal.

Overcome with anguish, the stepmother rushed to find her stepdaughter. "The dragon has taken your sister for its supper!" she cried. "Take the magic bow the crone gave you and go and save her."

Immediately the girl saddled her horse and rode into the wild mountains where the dragon had its lair. The ground before the entrance was littered with the bones and armor of its victims and in the middle lay the dragon, fast asleep. The girl gathered all her courage and crept past the snoring beast as quietly as she could. Deep in the cave, she could hear the desperate cries of her stepsister, whom the dragon had locked in a cage.

But the dragon was only pretending to be asleep and when it heard the girl approaching it gave a terrifying roar, flew up into the air, and prepared to pounce on the intruder and devour her. The girl took an arrow from the quiver she carried, drew

the magic bow and aimed at the dragon. The arrow flew fast and true, straight into the dragon's heart and the beast tumbled to earth, stone dead. The girl ran to the cage and freed her stepsister, then taking the tip of the dragon's tail as proof it was dead, the sisters mounted the horse and returned to the kingdom.

There was joy throughout the land when the people saw the dragon's tail end and realized that the terrifying monster was dead. The girl was brought before the king, who reminded her that he would reward her in any way she wanted. The young woman said quite simply, "Your majesty, I want to be queen." And so it came about that she and the king were married, and a wedding feast was held, and they lived together happily ever after.

Chapter 5

The Four Brothers

Once upon a time, there was a poor farmer and his wife. They tried their hardest to scratch a living from the land, which was full of thistles and rocks and had very thin, patchy soil. The weather was also unpredictable: sometimes it did not rain for months on end; sometimes it did not stop raining for weeks at a time. The farmer and his wife worked very hard but they often went to bed hungry, so that their children had enough to eat.

The farmer and his wife had four sons. They all grew up to be clever, handsome, and healthy but they were all very different. The oldest son was quiet and studious. He watched the birds, animals and insects at work and learned how the flowers, trees and crops grew. He often pointed out to the others things that they had not noticed. The second son was very good with his hands. He could make tools and furniture, and mend anything that was broken. The third son was cheerful and very strong. He often saw ways he and his brothers could work together to help make the farm more productive. The youngest son was sharp-sighted and quick thinking. He was a good hunter and often brought home meat to supplement the family's meager meals.

When the brothers were old enough to stand on their own two feet, their father said to them, "My sons, the time has come for you to leave us. You know that life on the farm is hard. The soil is thinner and poorer than ever, the yield is less every year and the cows are giving no milk. Your mother and I can no longer feed you all. Each of you, go and find a trade, so that you can make your own way in the world."

The four brothers were saddened by their father's words but they knew he was right. So, they took what few belongings

they had, bade their parents farewell, and set out on their journey into the wide, wide world.

At first, all four brothers traveled together, across mountains and through valleys, until they reached a crossroads in a forest so dense and so dark that the sun could barely be seen through the leaves and branches. The brothers stopped and stared at the four different paths that led away in different directions, until the oldest said, "This is a sign that we must separate and follow whatever destiny has decided for us. But let us promise to return to this spot four years hence and see what we have become."

The brothers embraced, then each went on his way. Soon after he had set off on his path, the oldest brother met a stranger who stopped him and asked who he was and where he was going. The oldest brother replied, "I am the oldest of four and I am searching for what I can best be in the world." When he said this, the stranger replied, "Come with me and I will make you a glassworker. You will make lenses that will help you see the tiniest things on earth and the furthest objects in the sky. Nothing will ever be hidden from you." As he listened to the stranger, the oldest son realized that being a glassworker would suit him very well, and decided to follow him.

The second son's path took him to a village where he met a stranger who stopped him to ask who he was and where he was going. The second son replied, "I am the second of four and I am searching for what I can best be in the world." When he said this, the stranger replied, "Come with me and I will make you a blacksmith. It is hard work but if you become my apprentice you will learn how to work any metal on Earth and make anything anybody wants or needs. I will teach you how to do beautiful and detailed work that will take people's breath away." As he listened to the stranger, the second son realized that being a blacksmith would suit him very well, and decided to follow him.

In his turn the third brother also met a stranger, a sooty, jolly person who blocked the path he was following. "Who are you and where are you going?" laughed the stranger. Like the others, the third brother replied, "I am the third of four and I am searching for what I can best be in the world." The stranger said, "Become a chimney sweep, like me! I am no ordinary chimney sweep. With me, you will scale greater heights than anybody else. You will climb and twist and leap and bound and the people who see you will be amazed and demand to learn how to do the same." As he listened, the third son realized that being a chimney sweep would suit him very well, and decided to follow him.

The path the youngest brother followed took him deep into the forest until he arrived at a sunlit glade where a stranger stood. This stranger asked the same question, to which he replied, "I am the youngest of four and I am searching for what I can best be in the world." "Come with me, said the stranger, "and I will teach you to be a huntsman. You will learn magical skills no other huntsman has ever learned. You will see birds and beasts no other huntsman has ever seen." As he listened, the youngest son realized that being a huntsman would suit him very well, and decided to follow him.

The four brothers each served four years as apprentices and did so well that their skills began to surpass those of their masters. When it was time for the oldest brother to leave, his master said, "I can teach you nothing more but I can give you something to remember me by and help you as you make your way in the world. With these magic lenses, nothing will ever be hidden from you, wherever you go." And he gave the first brother a pair of binoculars with the finest lenses the young man had ever seen.

The second brother had become an astonishing blacksmith. He could make or repair any object under the sun, and not just in metal. As he prepared to leave, his master told him, "You are the best apprentice I have ever had. I have something to give you to remember me by and help you as you make your way in the world. With this magic hammer you will perform wonders with whatever you lay your hands on." And he gave the second brother a hammer that was as light as air but as solid as rock.

As for the third brother, after four years there was no height that he was unable to scale as nimbly as a mountain goat and as fearlessly as an eagle. "Now you can climb even higher and faster than me!" said his master. "Time you were off, my boy. I have something to give you to remember me by and help you make your way in the world." And taking his own boots off his feet, he said, "Take these magic boots. When you wear them you will be able to climb anywhere you want to go. You will never fall and nobody will be able to stop you or catch you."

After four years, the youngest brother had become a highly accomplished huntsman. When the time came for him to leave, his master handed him a magnificent gun and said, "With this magic gun no animal will be able to hide from you and there is no beast you need fear. Wherever you aim, this gun will find its mark. And while you bear this gun, whatever you set out to do, you will succeed in doing."

As luck would have it, the four brothers arrived at the same time at the crossroads where they had agreed to meet, embraced each other, and set off to return home. Their parents were delighted to see them all safe and sound and begged to hear the adventures they had had over the past four years. So the four brothers told them about the strangers they had met, and their curious apprenticeships, and the magic gifts each had been given on parting from their masters.

"Can this really be true?" said their father. "Let us see what you can do." Turning to the oldest brother, he said, "On that mountain yonder there will be a vulture sitting on a ledge. Can you see it?" The oldest son took out his magic binoculars and immediately located the bird. His father began to grow excited. "Is the bird sitting on any eggs?" he asked. Again, his son raised his binoculars, and said, "It is sitting on three eggs." His father's eyes began to shine. "All my life I have heard that those eggs have magic powers. It is said that if you bury those eggs in the soil, the land will be fertile until the end of time. I know many farmers who have tried to get those eggs but none have succeeded. If anyone comes close to the cliff, the vulture pecks out their eyes."

"Leave this to me," said the youngest brother, and he took out his magic gun, aimed at the bird, and fired. Immediately, the vulture tumbled from the cliff. His father danced with happiness. "But how will we fetch the eggs?" he cried. "Nobody has ever been able to scale that cliff." Even as he was talking, the second brother had pulled out his magic hammer and begun to work. Within seconds he had fashioned an ingenious ladder from the bits and bobs that lay around him. Their father clapped his hands with delight. "But who will dare to climb that ladder?" he said. "Even if it holds, it will be impossible to reach the nest." "Nonsense!" laughed the third brother and pulling on his magic boots he scampered up the ladder, across the cliff face and onto the ledge where the vulture had made its nest, whistling all the time. Putting the eggs in his pocket, he leapt and swung back to the ground, where he handed the eggs, unbroken, to his father. His brothers cheered while the third son grinned and bowed and their father wept for joy.

"My boys," he said, "You spent your time well. You have each become the best you can be. You have learned to do great things and now you have shown that you can do even greater things together. I don't know whom to praise the most for getting me these eggs so I thank and bless you all equally. May you continue to use what you have learned for the better of us all." The farmer buried the vulture's eggs in the poor, thin soil of his land and from that day forward everything he planted yielded such an abundance of good things that he was able to share them with all his neighbors and no one went hungry again.

Not long after the brothers returned, there was great unrest in the kingdom. A savage wild boar began to terrorize the country, tearing up crops and killing the farmers when they tried to protect their land. Whoever crossed the boar's path was ripped open by its great, curved tusks. No spear or bullet could penetrate the skin of the enormous beast. Worse, the boar seemed to have supernatural powers. The few hunters who managed to creep up to it unharmed said it disappeared before their eyes and certainly before they could raise their gun or bow. People began to say that the boar was a wicked sorcerer that took on a boar's shape to terrify the people or an evil spirit that could never be killed. The king became desperate for a champion who would help rid his kingdom of the beast and offered his only daughter in marriage to whoever was able to kill it.

Soon the four brothers heard about the king's great prize. "Surely," said the third brother, "if we put all our great skills together we will be able to find and kill this beast." So they set off once again until, after many days of travel, they arrived at the edge of the forest where the boar was said to be hiding. Yet the boar was nowhere to be seen. Now, all four brothers had learned to be patient during the four long years of their apprenticeships but as the hours stretched into days and the boar still did not appear, they began to feel discouraged. Again, the third brother urged them on. "Don't be downhearted," he said. "I believe that together we will do what we set out to do. We will find and kill the boar and claim the king's reward."

Cheered by his words, the oldest brother raised the magic lenses to his eyes, saying, "I will try one more time to see if I can find the beast." Just as he spoke, he caught a movement and cried out to his brothers, "It is there! I have seen where it entered the forest!" and he began to lead his brothers in the right direction.

As night was falling, the four brothers set up camp close to the place where the beast had been seen to wait until daylight. While they waited, the second brother said, "No bullet has been

able to kill the beast. With my hammer I will make some magic bullets that I am sure will pierce its hide." And he set to work. As light broke, the third brother said, "I will climb to the top of the highest tree to see where the boar has its lair." And he sprang up into the treetops and was soon out of sight. When he returned only seconds later, he said, "I have seen the boar not far from here but it is lying in such thick undergrowth that it is unapproachable." "Never fear," said the youngest brother, "while I bear this gun we cannot fail to find it and no animal I have hunted yet has gotten away from me." So saying, he took the magic bullets the second brother had made and followed the trail his brothers had found.

The youngest brother moved so silently that even the birds roosting in the trees didn't notice him passing. Eventually, he came to a gloomy hollow that led to the watering hole and lair of the savage beast. The youngest brother was so close that he could smell the boar and hear its heavy breathing. Slowly, he crawled closer and closer, until he was almost on top of the beast. When the boar saw the youngest brother, it rushed toward him with foaming jaw and whetted tusks, to kill him as it had done all the others. But the youngest brother shouldered his unusual gun, pulled the trigger, and shot the boar through the heart. With a great bellow, the boar fell thrashing to the ground and for a while everything in the forest seemed to tremble. Then the beast was no more.

The second brother cut out the boar's enormous tusks to prove to the king that the boar was indeed dead. When the four brothers returned to the court with their trophies, there was great rejoicing.

But the king faced a dilemma. "My dear young men," he said. "I promised my daughter in marriage to the man who killed the boar. Which of you is most deserving of her?"

The four brothers stared at each other, dismayed. None of them spoke for a while, and then finally the oldest brother said, "Without my magic lenses we would never have found the beast." The third brother said, "If I hadn't climbed the highest tree, we would never have found its lair. And without my encouragement, you might have given up our quest." The second brother said, "Only my magic bullets could penetrate the boar's hide." And the youngest brother said, "I tracked the boar to its lair and shot it through the heart. Only I killed the boar."

The king's daughter was listening carefully to what they said and spent some time in deep thought. Then she turned to the youngest brother and said, "You tracked and killed the boar but you could not have done so without your brothers' magic bullets, magic lenses, strength and encouragement. None of you on his own could have killed the beast. It was only by working together that you were able to accomplish this great feat. Because each of you have an equal claim to me, none of you shall have me. Instead, I ask that my father give each of you a dukedom, with great, rich landholdings."

The four brothers saw sense in what the princess said. They moved to their dukedoms, where they continued to use their extraordinary skills for all who asked them for help, married four charming and deserving wives, and lived happily ever after.

Chapter 6

King Lion and the Bonobo

Once upon a time, in a land far, far away, there was a forest where no human being had ever set foot, and where there were only animals. Although the animals lived together harmoniously, the forest was a scene of chaos. Fruit and vegetables were harvested too early or too late. Rocks and logs clogged the rivers, choking the fish. Trees fell down without warning, endangering the lives of birds and animals. The time had come, many of the animals thought, to choose a ruler who would establish order in the forest and lead the animal kingdom. But who would be best for the job? All the animals had different ideas and many thought they would make the best candidate. The arguments rolled on and on until the screeching, chattering, roaring, and whistling became a cacophony of noise that filled the forest.

Eventually, the porcupine rattled his quills until he had silence and said, "Let's hold a competition. Any animal that thinks it would be a good ruler should give a short speech explaining why it should be chosen. After the speeches, we will have a vote and the animal with the most votes will be crowned ruler of the forest."

All the animals thought this was an excellent idea and those that wanted to be chosen began to think long and hard about what they could say to convince the others.

When the time for the competition had arrived, the bear was the first to step forward. "There is no question that I should be king. I am big, I am strong, I have magnificent jaws, I can climb trees, I can dig holes in the earth and I can swim. Because I can do all these things, I am the obvious choice." But the other animals murmured among themselves, "Yes, he can do all these things-but he is not very clever."

Now it was the turn of the giraffe, who said, "I am the tallest. No animal has a neck and legs as long as mine. I have a tongue longer than any of you. I can reach the leaves on the highest trees. Clearly, I should be queen." But the other animals said to each other, "All she's got is a long neck and long legs-that's not enough."

The elephant was next in line. He said, "I am the biggest, heaviest, and noisiest of you all. I have beautiful ivory tusks, I can push down trees, and I can tear down branches. Wherever I go, the earth trembles. You should choose me as your king." This time the murmuring among the other animals was kinder. "He's not just big," they said. "He has a brain as well."

But as their voices rose approvingly, the lion muscled his way forward and the animals grew quiet. "Enough of this nonsense," said the lion. "You have all watched me hunt. You have all seen my teeth and my claws and heard me roar. I am the most magnificent animal in the forest. I am already the king of beasts. Who else can you choose as your ruler?"

After the lion had spoken, there was a long silence before the animals began to speak again. Some said, "Lions are killers. He might eat us, not lead us." Others said, "He is very fond of the sound of his own voice. He won't listen to any of us." But most said, "I don't want to find myself at the wrong end of those teeth and claws," and out of fear the animals cast their votes for the lion and he became king of the forest.

If any of the animals had hoped that the lion would prove to be a good leader, they were mistaken. Nothing changed in the forest. The crops continued to fail, the rivers remained blocked,

and trees fell faster than ever. Worse, the harmony that the animals had enjoyed now disappeared. Instead there was anxiety and fear, because, as some of them had foretold, the lion turned out to be a very cruel and unpredictable ruler with a ravenous appetite. Once he became king, he began killing and eating many of the smaller animals in the forest.

So afraid were the animals that none of them dared to say anything to the king. Although he held daily court, the lion did all the talking. Nobody disagreed with him, as questioning the king was very dangerous. All he cared about was having a full stomach. Whenever he pounced on and ate an unfortunate victim, the lion's excuse was that the animal had made a mistake, and mistakes of any kind were not allowed. After a while, the lion was killing so many of his fellow animals that he could no longer claim to be hungry. Instead, he had learned to enjoy killing for killing's sake. Now no animal in the kingdom was safe, from the smallest mouse to the mightiest elephant.

So dire was the animals' plight that one day the timid dik-dik antelope summoned the courage to call a secret meeting of all the animals. When they were gathered together, she said, "We wanted a ruler who would make the forest a better place but we made a terrible mistake in choosing the lion. He terrorizes and exploits us and has killed and eaten hundreds of our friends. We must stop him, but how?"

The wise pygmy chimpanzee, the bonobo, spoke up, saying, "We are many and the lion is only one. If we all pull together we can throw him out of the forest."

This was too much for the other animals, who were too afraid to attempt to overthrow the lion. But they agreed that the bonobo could go to the king and plea for mercy towards the other animals in the forest, so the bonobo set off for the lion's den.

Luckily, the lion, who was growing fatter and lazier by the day, had just eaten an unfortunate ostrich who had strayed into his sight, so he did not pounce on the bonobo as she approached. "What do you want, ape?" he growled.

The bonobo replied, "Your majesty, I am here to help you remember that a king does not need sharp teeth and claws and a mighty roar to rule wisely. A good king rules with compassion and humility. He makes sure his subjects are happy and safe. I beg you to stop killing and have mercy on your subjects."

The lion snarled with fury. "How dare you address your king in this way!" he roared. "You're lucky my belly is too full for me to move, otherwise, I would kill and eat *you* right here and now."

The bonobo returned to the disappointed animals, having failed in her mission, and another meeting was held. The discussions continued long into the night until finally the hare said that she had a plan that might improve their lives. "The king enjoys killing so much that soon there will not be enough of us left to eat and he will starve to death. But he is also growing fat and lazy. I propose that we draw lots each day and whoever is so unlucky to be the "winner" will be a meal for the king. This way, more of us will be saved and we can control the king's appetite and his anger." It was a terrible proposal but none of the animals could think of a better plan and they all agreed to put it to the king.

That night, all the animals of the forest gathered in front of the lion's den. As they drew near, they could hear him gnawing

on his latest victim, a fat kudu antelope who had been so busy grazing it had not heard the lion creep up behind. The hare hopped carefully towards the lion, who licked his lips at the prospect of an additional evening snack. But just as he raised a huge paw, the hare said, "Your majesty, please hear me out. We have a plan that will make your life easier and mean that you will never need to hunt again." And the hare explained the terrible plan she had devised to make sure the lion had a daily meal.

The lion didn't think it was a terrible plan at all. He very much liked the idea. His dinner would come to him instead of his having to go out and get it and he would have even less to do. Ruling the kingdom was tiresome enough already. The hare's plan would give him more time to laze in the sun and sleep. So the lion said, "I agree to your proposal but be sure that my dinner comes to me by sunset every day, otherwise I'll kill all of you."

After that, the animals in the forest held a lottery every day to determine who would be the lion's dinner and every day at sunset the poor animal would walk into the lion's den to be eaten.

Although life in the forest became predictable the animals were far from happy. Their terrible plan gave them more control but all of them lived in fear that their turn would surely come. Once the daily draw was over, and the next victim chosen, the other animals would slink away in misery and tremble in fear for the rest of the day and night.

The lion, on the other hand, was delighted with the arrangement. He no longer had to crawl around and hunt for his food. Now his dinner walked right up to meet him. Consequently, he grew fatter and fatter and lazier and lazier and meanwhile the crops still failed, the rivers were still choked, and the trees of the forest fell all around him.

Nevertheless, the animals preferred their chosen misery to the alternative, and had no further thoughts of trying to overthrow King Lion until the day came when the bonobo was chosen to be his next meal. The bonobo didn't seem upset, as some other animals had been; neither was she in a hurry to have it over and done with, as others had felt. Instead, she busied herself in the forest, deliberately delaying her arrival, and did not arrive at the lion's den until long after sunset. By then, the lion was in a very foul mood.

When he saw the bonobo, the lion bellowed, "Why have you kept me waiting so long? I could kill all of you for this!" The bonobo replied, "My deepest apologies, your majesty, but it is not my fault I am late. A lion was chasing me and wanted to eat me for dinner. I thought there was no other lion in the forest and I was astonished-why, sire, I believe he is even bigger, fiercer, and has a much louder roar than your majesty."

"What?" roared the lion. "Another lion has dared enter my forest? Where is he? I will tear him to pieces!"

The bonobo said, "I will show you the way and you shall see for yourself." And she set off, followed by the lion. They padded through the forest until they arrived at a deep well. The bonobo pointed to it, and said, "This is the place where the lion lives, your majesty. I believe it is hiding inside."

The lion crept up and looked down into the depths of the well. There, to his great surprise, he saw another lion. The sight made him furiously angry and he roared, and roared, and roared. But the other lion seemed to roar back even louder, as

the king's voice echoed round the well. Provoked beyond endurance, the lion king pounced on his reflection, fell deep into the well, and drowned.

When the bonobo returned, the other animals were terrified to see that she was still alive. Hadn't the king sworn to kill them all if he did not have his dinner? But when the bonobo told them how her trick had worked, and that the lion king was drowned and gone forever, they cheered and praised her cleverness. Then the porcupine rattled his quills until there was silence and said, "My friends, we wanted a ruler who would be clever, and look after us, and keep us safe. We made the wrong choice once, out of fear. Let us make the right choice now, with what we can see with our own eyes and hear with our own ears. I propose the bonobo should be our queen." All the other animals agreed unanimously.

"Thank you, my friends," said the bonobo. "From today I decree that there shall be no more killing in the forest. Tonight, let us celebrate our freedom from the tyranny of King Lion. But tomorrow I will hold court and invite every one of you to tell me what you think should be done to make our life in the forest better. I promise I will listen to what you have to say and that in as short a time as possible our land will bear ripe fruit and vegetables, our rivers will run clear and free, and our trees will grow tall and strong."

And just as the Bonobo Queen had promised, in no time at all life in the forest was transformed. Every animal was heard, from the tiniest shrew to the bulkiest rhinoceros, and all worked together to put the land to rights. The forest prospered and everything that grew and worked within it lived happily ever after.

About the Author

Manfred Kets de Vries is among the world's top fifty leading management thinkers and one of the most influential contributors to human resource management. He is the author, co-author, or editor of more than 40 books and has published over 400 scientific papers as chapters in books and as articles. Furthermore, he has written over a hundred case studies, including six that received the Best Case of the Year Award. His books and articles have been translated into thirty-one languages. He is a member of seventeen editorial boards and has been elected a Fellow of the Academy of Management. Kets de Vries has been given many honors, including Lifetime Achievement Awards in the US and Germany. He is also the recipient of two honorary doctorates.

Manfred is the Distinguished Clinical Professor of Leadership Development and Organizational Change at INSEAD. He is also the Raoul de Vitry d'Avaucourt Emeritus Professor of Human Resource Management. He received an economics degree from the University of Amsterdam and a MBA and DBA from the Harvard Business School. He is a practicing psychoanalyst/psychotherapist and a member of the Canadian Psychoanalytic Society, The Paris Psychoanalytic Society, and the International Psychoanalytic Association.

Manfred was the first fly fisherman in Outer Mongolia and is a member of New York's Explorers Club. In his spare time he can be found in the rainforests or savannas of Central Africa, the Siberian taiga, the Pamir and Altai Mountains, Arnhemland, or within the Arctic Circle.